good deed rain

Books by Allen Frost

Ohio Trio
Bowl of Water
Another Life
Home Recordings
The Mermaid Translation
The Selected Correspondence of Kenneth Patchen
The Wonderful Stupid Man
Saint Lemonade
Playground
Roosevelt
5 Novels
The Sylvan Moore Show
Town in a Cloud
A Flutter of Birds Passing Through Heaven:
A Tribute to Robert Sund
At the Edge of America
Lake Erie Submarine
The Book of Ticks
I Can Only Imagine
The Orphanage of Abandoned Teenagers
Different Planet
Go with the Flow: A Tribute to Clyde Sanborn
Homeless Sutra
The Lake Walker
A Hundred Dreams Ago
Almost Animals
The Robotic Age

The ROBOTIC AGE

ALLEN FROST

The Robotic Age ©2018
Allen Frost, Good Deed Rain
Bellingham, Washington
ISBN 978-1-64370-398-5

Writing: Allen Frost
Cover & Chapter Illustrations:
  Aaron Gunderson
Cover Production Assistance:
  Fred Sodt
Apple: TFK!

The Frost apartment directly overlooked the Spire, as did the apartments of all Committee Secretaries. Allen took a reassuring breath and then climbed the stairs.

—Philip K. Dick, *The Man Who Japed*

The
ROBOTIC AGE
ALLEN FROST

THE CHAPTERS

INTRODUCTION

The Robotic Age wishes to thank two friends for their contributions to this book.

First, I'm indebted to The Great Rob Millis. We had a weekly school radio show, invading Maine with skipping records and mad story scenarios spun on the spot. Later, we would record comedy adventures on tape featuring a cannibal explorer, detectives, tin can aliens, a vampire who played ragtime, pirates, tractors and a one-legged magician named Marconi. It's an astounding achievement that Marconi has hobbled out of the airwaves to land in his very own book.

Also, thanks to The Mighty Aaron Gunderson for more inspiration and the amazing illustrations that bring this story to life. It's true that Aaron could have been heir to the actual Cronco Cooler fortune, had the company not gone under. (There are rumors that the Cronco cooler had a design flaw that made it overheat. Too bad for those picnics in the 1950s that ended with melted ice cream).

And now, the lights are dimming...on stage, our story is just beginning.

—AF

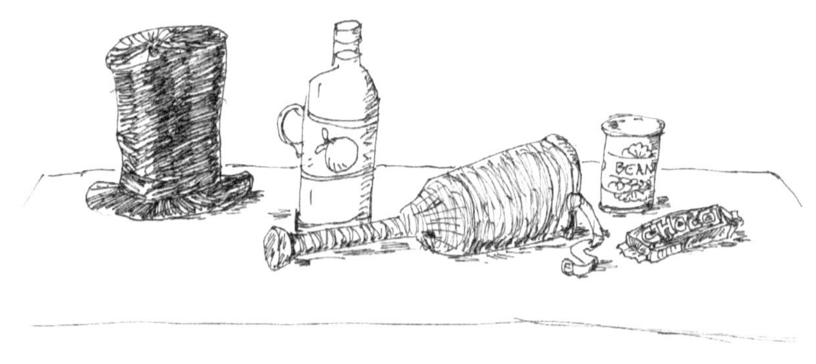

BEAN
CHOCO

1) The Great Marconi

The Great Marconi leaned on the kitchen table and unscrewed his leg. He wobbled and lifted the heavy hollow limb and emptied out the contents: a few cans of soup, some vegetables, a bag of rice and a carton of orange juice. He held the leg upright from the ankle and shook out a candy bar. Dessert. Every act, even this one, should end with one last spectacle.

2) Shoplifting

He put the food away. He felt bad about using magic this way, but what could he say? He had to eat. Money was tight so he had to use his talents to make ends meet. What choice did he have? Hadn't he suffered enough for his art? Anyway, it wasn't much. A couple times a week he would go to Food Giant and shoplift. He had never been caught. Time had passed but he was still The Great Marconi.

3) The North Pole

Stuck to the white door of the fridge was a sort of window. It was a cold view, a porthole to a bleak world. An empty arctic—at least there should have been the orange juice carton he just put in there—but it wasn't a window. It was a postcard from the North Pole.

4) Big News

That postcard was the reason Marconi spent the morning cleaning his apartment, went grocery shopping, and why he was about to leave for the bus station. The postcard was big news. In only an hour, his old friend would be back in town.

5) Magic

Back in the day, when The Great Marconi performed on stage, he would have been pleased with a crowd this size. Even at that fateful matinee when he sawed his own leg off, there were only three people in the audience. And two of them were asleep. Yes, he still had the bug and with some time before the bus arrived at the station, the thought did cross his mind—he had a deck of cards in his pocket—magic was never that far behind.

6) Elixir

Cronco and Marconi had a medicine show act for a year after Marconi's accident, selling Youth Elixir. Using a cane to hobble on stage, Marconi would drink a fair amount of it for the audience then remove his top hat to show his gray hair had turned dark again. Alas, they didn't sell much of the stuff. And although it didn't actually work as a youth serum, all that ingestion did have an unintended side effect on Marconi—every once in a while down the years, unexpectedly, he would turn invisible. It was never for long and since there was no way of knowing when it would happen, he couldn't plan on using it to his advantage. One moment he would be gone. The next moment he would be back.

for the audience

7) Golden Retriever

Marconi didn't like sitting for too long. It was almost as if that phantom leg of his was standing there, watching him with golden retriever eyes, waiting for a walk. He sighed and stood. He could almost hear that leg nearby, wagging and tap dancing across the crowded bus station floor.

8) Whales

Outside, a cement platform ran like a pier and the buses came and went like whales. Marconi stood beside a pillar and watched. He used to keep cigarettes in his cuffs for moments like this. He watched the buses and felt like some old mariner on the dock where the whales would plow up out of the sea to see him. They greeted him with big round shiny eyes and wide flashing silver mouths. This one came from down the coast in California, another from even further, while he waited, a one-legged Ahab, for the one from Alaska.

nobody could see you

9) Invisible

Travelers passed him pulling bags, with children in tow or hopping around, hurried anxious blurs and chatters, and before he knew it, Marconi was invisible. What a time for him to fade from view. The bus was due any minute. It was strange knowing you were there, but nobody could see you. He had to step aside for a porter pushing a steamer trunk.

10) A Glass of Water

It might have been Marconi's greatest act, but it wasn't magic at all. So what if he went unnoticed? He was less than a glass of water. He was only standing in a tide that pushed and pulled and he waited to wash back. It didn't take long. The big clock on the pillar behind him made a loud click and he reappeared on the platform just as a dusty bus from Alaska turned off the street.

11) The Land of Snow

With a great sigh, the tired bus stopped against the curb. As Marconi made his way towards it, the door hissed open. He had already seen the routine with other buses, but now it was new: soon his old friend would be revealed. Marconi stood in the patch of shade where a pigeon had been and watched the driver hurry out to open the first cargo hatch. There were three of them below the row of tinted windows. He slung the bags out onto the cement while Marconi turned his attention back to the door. Marconi didn't expect Cronco to be the first one off. He was probably in the back row, hemmed in by shadows, the last to emerge from the land of snow.

12) Rocket Ship

What a rocket ship ride. It was funny to think how far away these people had been. Marconi observed every one. The looks on their faces each told a story. What had they left behind? What were they going to do next? Was this their new home, or were they just passing through? Finally, the bus was empty. The very last passenger was an old woman carrying a birdcage.

13) Distance

"There's nobody else on my bus," the driver told Marconi.

"You're sure? He's not—"

"Nobody," the driver repeated and, before Marconi could say something more, he pulled a lever near the dashboard. The door clapped shut. The bus gave a snort, engine growling, and the driver tapped the horn once as the whale-like shape backed out into the bay.

It left a big space in the air.

Marconi could see a chain-link fence, tall yellow weeds, a parking lot, a brick alley between buildings that framed a slice of distance with a railroad track.

something called

14) Telepathic

Something called to him from all that distance—not a megaphone, not a radio signal
or telepathic message—it was a flash of metal,
bright as a star. And in that instant, Marconi
had the feeling he knew exactly who it was.

15) Hush

Cronco saw the notice a year ago—or was it longer? It was hard to tell when time slipped past you like water. As Marconi left the bus lot, he corrected his thought—Cronco saw the notice some time ago: a lighthouse needed a keeper. The lighthouse was far away from magical mishaps and cheap elixirs, matinees and children's birthday parties. The lighthouse was at the North Pole. It still sounded strange to Marconi. A lighthouse at the North Pole? But Cronco didn't think twice. He bought a ticket and was gone. So much for an audience, so much for their act…The sound of the stage quickly faded to a hush. Time passed. Marconi got by…Things could have been better. As maybe it was meant to be, magic seemed a thing of the past…until the postcard arrived.

16) Logic

Cronco waited in the open door of a box-car, like a hobo between the Northern Pacific yin yang logo and a Great Northern car with a circled mountain goat. He waved as Marconi neared and finally he called out hello. The sound sent a blackbird flying. What's he doing on a train? Marconi wondered. But he was sure there would be some logical explanation…with Cronco there always was.

17) All the Tin Cans in the World

"Cronco!" Marconi smiled as he picked his way carefully among the stones near the track. It was so funny to see his old friend transported through time. "Why weren't you on the bus?"

"I calculated that the train would be faster. It was. I arrived here at dawn."

Marconi smiled. Still the same old Cronco. But he could see there was a problem. He knew enough about acrobats and show-stopping acts to see that Cronco was in a predicament. How was Cronco supposed to get down from the boxcar? It was a five foot drop to the ground. Cronco wasn't exactly made for that fall. It would sound like all the tin cans in the world hitting the yard.

18) Egypt

"You can't get down, can you?" Marconi asked.

Cronco couldn't deny it. When he stepped onto the train from a rainy platform in Fairbanks, he never expected this to happen. He held his silver arms outstretched and said, "If I only had the wings of a dove."

Marconi nodded, "Looks like it's my turn to help you out of a jam." He spun on his good heel. Was there a forklift somewhere? Did someone leave the keys in a pickup truck?

"A block and tackle would be most useful," Cronco said. "A winch and pulley set. Remember how they moved those pyramids in ancient Egypt?"

But as Marconi hobbled out among the tracks and weeds and broken glass, he was remembering something not quite so lost in history.

a simple illusion

19) Thrills & Fanfare

The Great Marconi didn't like the memory. He could feel the saw still held tightly in his hand. The rasping sound of its teeth had stopped and there was a long moment of silence before his leg thumped to the stage. How could such a simple illusion go so wrong? All over America magicians sawed their assistants in half. Thrills and fanfare. There was nothing to it. He had seen the diagrams in *Popular Mechanics*. He remembered the curtain coming down as Cronco steamed over to save his life. So yes, he owed that robot a favor. It was the least he could do—a one-legged man limping around the rail yard in search of wood scrap to make a ramp.

20) The Locomotive Escape

Eventually an angle formed from some planks, a pallet, a plywood sheet. Marconi hoped it would be enough. He was exhausted. He ran a handkerchief across his face and asked, "What do you think?" It looked like a splintery nursery rhyme, a shipwreck at a slant.

Cronco disappeared into the boxcar shadows and returned with a big metal cooler. The last time Marconi saw it, Cronco was lugging it off to the North Pole. It was sort of his suitcase—a suitcase for someone who never needed a change of clothes or a toothbrush.

The dragonflies looked down zigzag paths above. All the scene lacked was a snare drum roll in the orchestra pit and a voice presenting the long awaited return of The Great Marconi and Cronco, the Mighty Automaton, in the death-defying Locomotive Escape.

21) Penny Nails

If you blinked you might have missed it. Fortunately, the show is repeated in playgrounds across the country, wherever there is a slide and children. With the cooler on his lap, Cronco slid down the ramp. Marconi gave him a hand standing up. That was it. The dragonflies drifted away.

"Welcome back!" Marconi said and patted the robot's shoulder.

Cronco shook his head. It sounded like a bag of penny nails. "Thank you," he said. "It's good to be home."

Another train moaned in the distance, the rumble of all its wheels crumpling the air like a dream.

22) Everything Is Everywhere

They only got as far as the fence on the edge of the rail yard when someone called out to them. "Where do I find everything?" He looked like he had crawled off a train too, carrying a backpack and a look of dust and miles of planetary unrest.

"I don't know," Marconi answered with a sort of laugh. What a question! He tried to keep walking but Cronco had stopped. It was too late, they were drawn in.

"What are you looking for?" the robot said. "Everything is everywhere."

"Oh no," Marconi groaned. It was happening again. They had been through this act before. Two friends brought together can create a circuit switch and even just walking down the street, Marconi and Cronco would be played for the amusement of some unseen force wielding fields of energy to create situations stocked with characters sent from some bizarre central casting. They were back on stage. It was all around them. The whole world circled them and they were pressed like two batteries put back in a long disused toy contraption that now began to whir and spark and grab.

back on stage

41

23) Goodwill

The Eleanor Rigby Apartments looked like they were still under construction. Although it had been there for years, it was a building that couldn't pay its own reality. There were gaps where the blue sky showed. Framed between trees and telephone poles, it could have poured out of a cardboard box onto the corner of Forest Street like a puzzle bought at a Goodwill store. It wasn't until after you spent half the afternoon putting it together that you realized there were missing pieces, random lost edges and jagged undone shapes a song could whisper through.

24) Yesterday

A big section of the wall had been erased. The sounds from three stories down carried up and a breeze blew into the room.

"That is unfortunate architecture," said Cronco. He took a few steps into the apartment as Marconi hurried towards the missing wall. "Be careful."

"Is this rent day?" Marconi hobbled into the bright sunlight. He rubbed his forehead. "Or was it yesterday? Yes," he answered himself, "it must have been yesterday." The weight of that last word was too much. He collapsed into the chair that now had a bird's eye view of the town. He shrugged. "I thought it was today"

Cronco clicked and creaked a little closer.

"Don't worry," Marconi said, with his eyes closed, "I'll pay the manager in a minute. Then we'll have our wall back." He yawned. "I need to rest first." His hand reached for a plaid blanket on the floor and he pulled it up and over into sleep.

from dream to dream

25) Imagined Television

Pigeons woke Marconi. He twitched his foot and their cooing stopped. They quickly left the ledge and flapped off loudly. If he didn't get up too and pay, he knew more of his apartment would disappear. It wasn't so bad in the summer. He could let a few days slip by. Last summer he slept with no walls around him at all. He liked it. If there wasn't a roof he could have been camping. It was another story in the winter though. That's when rent meant something.

A gentle breeze combed the room and brushed the newspaper leaves on the kitchen table.

Marconi turned in his chair and saw Cronco sitting on his cooler, head slumped, still sleeping. He wondered what that robot was dreaming. What kind of world was created in that metal head? Marconi imagined television. A tall aerial somewhere was broadcasting shows. Cronco experienced other worlds that could flick from dream to dream.

26) Ragtime

The door had a nameplate on it that read MANAGER. Marconi rapped twice and he and Cronco waited. Behind the door, a piano played ragtime, not very well, haltingly. It stopped midsong. Marconi felt his fist curl. He didn't like confrontations. His phantom leg was running away.

With a snap sudden as a rattrap, the door yanked open and the manager glared at Marconi. "Did you forget something?"

"Yes, yes," Marconi fumbled, "You see, although my rent is overdue—"

"Who's that with you?" the manager croaked in a voice that had dropped twenty degrees. All of a sudden he was seeing a monster.

Cronco hummed and held his welded arm out.

The manager took a step backwards. "Is this your hired muscle?"

"What?" Marconi stared.

"Are you threatening me? Is this some kind of threat?"

Marconi patted his coat pocket. "I assure you, I—"

But the manager had retreated, pushed the

door until he looked through only a crack.

"I don't want any trouble!" With a rasping scratch he ran the chain lock into its track. One eye looked back. "I have bills to pay too, you know. I'm not looking for any trouble."

Marconi reached in his coat pocket for the check, but it was too much for the manager.

He was gone.

They were facing a shut door again, only now there was no ragtime…only an icy silence.

27) The Electric Memory

At the kitchen table, Marconi worked a piece of wire over in his hands, bending it back and forth until it was almost soft as yarn.

Twenty minutes since they left the panicked manager's room and he was still holding onto the electric memory of it. He thought this is how Cronco must be all the time. But how could a robot know the feeling of being human, what everyone had to go through just to get by? Cronco only buzzed with the mechanics of being alive.

"Do you think we should get an act going again?" Cronco wanted to know.

"I don't know. I haven't done much magic since you left." Marconi tapped his leg. He didn't mention his weekly performance at the Food Giant. Sooner or later that would come to an ugly end. "Anyway, I happen to have gainful employment already."

Marconi tied some bright tissue paper with the end of the wire. A few nimble twists and he held a flower. It was his job. The magic was still there. He had to make 200 tonight.

the feeling of being human

A cardboard flat was filling with flowers. The radio was on, playing the sort of songs they don't play anymore. The walls were all where they should be and night was splashing around in the window. A peaceful American summer evening at home. Marconi asked the robot sitting across from him, "How was that lighthouse at the North Pole?"

Cronco had been studying the front page of the *Eleanor Echo* for an hour. Marconi was worried his gears had frozen. Then Cronco answered in a slow, flat voice, "Truthfully, there was no lighthouse."

"I thought you saw an ad in the paper?" Marconi held a half finished flower. "You said it was a lighthouse job at the North Pole."

Cronco shook his head.

Marconi was astounded. "Well, why on earth did you go all that way to the North Pole?"

"I heard something on the radio."

29) Clarence Andy

Before Marconi could ask about that radio message, Cronco rattled the newspaper and asked, "Who is this columnist for the *Echo*? His name is Clarence Andy."

"Oh brother," Marconi sighed. He set the flower aside. #83 could wait. "He's just a bad writer. The Eleanor has its own newspaper and he seems to get in each issue somehow. This is the only thing he could ever be published in. Those crackpot ideas and the bad grammar. Are you really reading that thing he wrote? Is that what you can't take your eyes off?"

Cronco nodded.

"Well, I'd like to hear what he wrote. Go ahead, read it aloud." Marconi chuckled, "If it's that important to a mind like yours, Clarence must be spinning pure gold."

somehow I knew where to go

I know it was danger to dive to the wreck of the Pelican. The portholes sparkled like mean eyes, telling me to turn around but I didn't. Plenty of bubbles hide me when I climed onto the deck and I walked on the seaweed covers. How or why I don't know but somehow I knew where to go. A door was a jar broken open on only a hinge left over. Am I afraid or just knowing something waits for me in there? What it was made me shout until my heart is screaming. A horibul ghost reached for me. I couldn't escape. "Get me off this ship!" it yelled. Then that ghost of dead sailer grabed me with both arms and shook me and I got cold everywhere. I had to fight it to crawl out of there. My air was running out and I don't know how I made it to shore in one pece. I opened my eyes only to see I didn't have the tresur I looked for. All I had was a white torn of cloth in my hand, riped off from that ghost.

31) Cronco's Dream

Of course robots have dreams—their minds never stop working. Cronco had a favorite dream he kept like a precious postage stamp. At night, with his circuits turned down, he liked to return to it. He was in a canoe. Marconi was there too. They were in a beautiful blue alpine lake surrounded by mountains and sky.

a favorite dream

currents that flowed

32) A Different River

That was all the rest Cronco needed. That dream took care of him. He woke ready to go. First, he scanned the room. Shadows clouded around. Marconi's box full of silhouette flowers waited on the table for morning. Cronco left the cooler he had been sitting on and walked over to the window.

Neon clung to the corners and black glass. The night carried on. It was a different river, with its own inhabitants, messages and music and currents that flowed.

For such a refrigerator on two feet, Cronco moved quietly, crossed the room and left with only a click of the apartment door.

33) A Familiar Road

A robot roaming the city streets was no cause for alarm in this day and age. Just the same, Cronco preferred the alleys or dark parking lots as he clunked and whirred his way down to the harbor. For light, a half moon and electricity here and there was alright, though he could see as well as an owl. Besides, he had taken this path before. It lived in his memory. Part of you stays on a familiar road if you've gone back and forth on it long enough.

34) The Wreck of the Polly Ann

Where the waves landed, the statue of a fisherman leaned above, holding a rope looped to throw out over one of the islands in the bay. The words on the pedestal were the names of crews lost at sea. For an hour, Cronco stood in front of it, absorbing it the same way as Clarence's newspaper story. Cronco knew three of those sailors and he knew the ship they sank on.

He had been on the deck of the Polly Ann when it was a wreck underwater. There was no lighthouse at the North Pole. Across hundreds of miles of land and icy depths of ocean, Cronco was called by the ghost on the ship's radio. He knew it meant danger to dive to the wreck of the Polly Ann, but danger never stopped him before.

35) To Be A Ghost

The bedroom door opened and footsteps walked in the apartment room. Someone bumped an invisible toe into the table and moaned. Marconi could see that Cronco was gone. It must have been close to dawn. The sound of Marconi continued over to the silver cooler parked against the wall. This was one of those times where being invisible would help to do something he knew he shouldn't. It would be so easy to lift the lid of that cooler and find out what a robot had to drag all the way from Alaska. The floorboards creaked as he neared it. Then he sighed long and sad. Is this what it meant to be a ghost—to roam around dark rooms making mischief?

36) The Flower Machine

In the morning light, the door was their alarm clock. Cronco's canoe vanished and he was sitting on his cooler instead.

The loud knocking brought Marconi hurrying from his bedroom. "It's Dobbs," he muttered, "here for the flowers." He grabbed the box on his way to the impatient door.

Cronco had not met Dobbs before, but he didn't like the sound of him.

Marconi fumbled the door open. "Mr. Dobbs! I thought it was you."

A man in a bowler hat and vest, drawn in quick charcoal lines, Dobbs got right to the point. "Is that 200?"

"As requested." Marconi presented the box, filled with twenty bundles of ten paper flowers. Crowded together, they shook and sighed as Dobbs whisked them away. There was something crow-like in the way he snatched the box and carried it off, almost flying down the hall.

"See you tomorrow, Mr. Dobbs!" Marconi called. He shut the door and mumbled, "Just a cog in the flower machine."

37) A Florida Tree

Like Old Mother Hubbard, there was little in Marconi's cupboard for his guest. But what did Cronco need? Not much. He was plugged into the outlet, recharging. So Marconi made do. A piece of toast. Some orange juice.

Marconi predicted another trip to the grocery today. Yes!—he took a sip from the cup and smiled—today Cronco would be with him! He wondered how much food that hollow robot could hide inside. It would be an amazing performance! Houdini was only locked up in water. A fish could do that. After they left Food Giant bare, the employees would stare in wonder…Nothing would be there. Not even the gum by the register. And back at the Eleanor, Cronco would be a vending machine, full as a factory, and Marconi would never go hungry again. It was incredible to imagine, but the longer he thought about it, he had to admit it was wrong to steal. That wasn't who they were; they were brought together for greatness.

Marconi looked at the juice in his cup. It could be traced back to a Florida tree, that came from a seed, that came from another seed, on and on in what really had to be the greatest magic ever. All that in a carton for only $2.99. The price of admission. Wasn't it worth it?

38) Hiding for Years

There was another knock at the door. This time Cronco answered it, sweeping it open.

"Is that Mr. Dobbs again?" Marconi called from the other room.

"No. Your apartment manager is here." Cronco added, "He may be petrified with fear."

Marconi looked for his coat, the one he wore yesterday with the rent check in the pocket. It hung from the kitchen door like half a scarecrow. "I'll be right there."

Cronco crowded the doorway and by the time Marconi arrived, the hall was empty.

"Where did he go?"

"He took off like a March hare," Cronco said.

"Which way?"

Cronco pointed a metallic claw.

Pulling his coat on, Marconi limped that way. He never thought he'd be chasing down the manager at rent time. Strange how the tables had turned…with one exception: Marconi knew where to look—the angle under the stairs, the laundry room closet, the garden in back of the building—he had been hiding for years.

39) Ultra Violet

Marconi didn't need ultra violet detection, sophisticated thermal or particulate sweeping equipment. He didn't even need a bloodhound at the end of a leash. He found the manager the first place he looked.

"Is that robot with you?" the manager said through the crack in the door.

"No, it's just me. Can I give you my rent?"

The door swung enough to see the manager and his piano. "Can we make a deal instead?"

"A deal?"

"I'll let you have free rent this month if you do me a favor."

Marconi held that thought aloft. It tipped and wobbled uncertainly.

"Two months rent free," the manager quickly bargained.

"What do you want me to do?"

40) Orson Welles

Two months of free rent! Marconi whistled up the stairs and down the hall to his room, moving with a spring in his step, almost as if his leg had never left him.

He was ready to sound like Orson Welles on the radio when he opened the apartment door.

But something a lot stranger than Martians landing in New Jersey was happening—Cronco had the cooler open and he stood beside it, holding up the outline of a person. It looked like someone cut from a cloud.

41) A New Illusion

To Marconi, everything was magic and this was no exception. Cronco folded the shape and stacked it back in the cooler, on top of a couple others. They were like shirts packed in a suitcase. The lid shut and Marconi instantly applauded. He was very impressed with Cronco the Mighty Automaton. The robot had brought back a new illusion from the North Pole, or wherever it was he had actually been.

"I would like to propose an errand for to-day," Cronco said matter-of-factly.

"Sure. The manager has a job for us tonight, but we've got all day." Marconi pointed at the cooler. "That looks like a real showstopper, what you were working on there."

"There was no lighthouse at the North Pole," said Cronco.

"Right. You told me that."

Cronco simulated a deep breath and said, "Before I left in such a hurry, I was collecting radio signals. They were from a ship in distress. After the Polly Ann sunk I continued to receive their S.O.S. Three men had gone down with the ship. They needed someone to rescue them."

"Right," Marconi nodded. "You had to help."

"It was not until I got there, until I went underwater and found the Polly Ann that I realized, they were already dead. There was a ghost at the radio transmitter. Two more ghosts were with him, waiting to go home."

Marconi pointed at the cooler again. "That's who you have in there?"

Cronco nodded. "I brought them back in cold storage. I promised to deliver them where they belong."

43) Lost Souls

"Did they tell you where to take them?"

Cronco said yes.

"Do they all live here in town?"

Cronco nodded again.

"So we're going to spend the day returning lost souls?"

"That is my plan."

"Alright," Marconi said. "I'll get my cane." It was hooked on the back of a chair by the window.

Cronco opened a hatch on his side. The curved door stayed open while he transferred handfuls of ice from the cooler into the compartment. That done, he carefully settled the stack of ghosts in their new home and shut the door.

Yes, Marconi thought, if only this whole routine had been seen on the stage; it would have made them a household name.

44) More Magic

"I was just imagining you on that boxcar with your cooler of ghosts, traveling all the way from Alaska." Marconi glanced at the limes placed in a green pyramid outside the bodega.

"Sometimes it was remarkable. Other times I had to turn myself off for long periods."

The limes passed them. Only a couple days ago, Marconi thought, he might have popped one into his sleeve. They were 79¢ apiece.

Suddenly Cronco stopped walking. He made a birdish sound as he put his hands to his belly.

"What's the matter?"

Cronco whispered, "I just felt them move."

"What? The ghosts?"

Cronco nodded. His fingers spread like flowers on his metal skin. He seemed to be gone from the sidewalk, the windows of shops, the sounds of cars on the street. Then he came back.

Marconi whispered, "You felt the ghosts move?"

45) The Electric Dog

After another block, they rested in the shade of a narrow tree. It was sort of an oasis on the sidewalk. Up in the green leaves, sparrows hopped. Marconi had the feeling Cronco never tired. He could rumble all over town like a taxi cab delivering ghosts.

They had a moment of calm before Cronco groaned, "Oh no…" A belated warning snapped along his memory circuit, but there wasn't time to retreat.

The old man and his orange electric dog saw them. "Look!" he cried. "We know who that is!" His jittery eyes were riveted on Cronco. "What a magnificent robot! What's his name again?"

"Cronco," Marconi said.

"Cronco! You're magnificent!" He pawed the robot while his electric dog circled and sparked. "We haven't seen you for quite a while. Where has he been?"

Marconi answered, "At the North Pole."

"Remarkable! That's remarkable. What were you doing there, Cronco?"

"Research," Cronco's flat voice replied.

"That's wonderful!" The old man released

his hold and turned to Marconi, "You're so lucky to have a robot this magnificent." He patted Cronco again.

"Okay," said Marconi. "Thanks."

"How old is he?"

Marconi said, "I don't know."

"I used to build these at the plant. There's not many of these still around. I'd sure like to get one of these to do everything for me. All I have is this electric dog. He gets my paper, that's about it."

"Okay," Marconi said, edging from the tree, "Well, we better go."

"A magnificent robot!" the old man crowed. And he called after them, "Let me know if you ever want to sell!"

46) Directions

On Cronco's flat open palm, a compass twitched and chirped. The needle revolved in the dial nervously.

"We're lost, aren't we?" said Marconi.

"I know where we have to go. I just do not know how to get there."

Marconi nodded, "That means we're lost." His leg was hurting too. He didn't often walk this far. "What's the name of that street again?"

"Hazel." Cronco gave the compass a shake.

"Let me go in here and ask for directions," Marconi hobbled off the sidewalk and opened the door of a coffee shop. The smell of the place revived him and gave him the strength to glide to a small round table by the window. The chair squeaked as it caught him. He reached in his coat pocket and used a handkerchief on his brow.

"What can I get for you?"

Marconi noticed the waiter, tall, white apron, open pad of paper, and asked for a coffee and, "Oh," he added, "maybe a sample of your wares."

"We have carrot cake."

"Splendid," Marconi brightened. Coffee

and cake suddenly became the only thing that mattered, written in big Broadway lights. Hazel Street slipped from sight. He forgot all about it until he turned and looked out the window.

Cronco stood out there surrounded by a blue crowd of girl scouts in uniform. They looked like water washing around him. They listened to him and then as one wave, all of them pointed excitedly to a place further on.

47) A Movie of Faces

The waiter watched Cronco stomp through the doorway. The bell above him was ringing like crazy and the shocked waiter dropped a full mug of coffee and a plate. They shattered. Cronco lumbered into the shop like a mechanical bull. It was a miracle he didn't cause more havoc as he turned stiffly on his way and stopped at Marconi's table.

"Excuse me." The waiter said, "Aren't you The Mighty Cronco?" He looked hypnotized.

Then he looked back at his customer seated by the window, "And you're Marconi!"

Solemnly, Marconi held up a hand. "The Great Marconi. Nice to meet you."

"Do you remember me?" the waiter asked.

Cronco ran a report in his mind. The memory banks showed a movie of faces until he stopped on one. He told the waiter, "We got you out of a tree when you were five. We have not seen you since that time."

Marconi lit up, "Oh, that's right! I remember Cronco held the ladder while I climbed to the top of that tree. You were stuck and afraid of falling. I had to carry you to the ground."

The waiter was over the moon seeing them

again after so long. Those were the days when there were heroes like that. Then he called out to the cook in the kitchen, "A new cup of coffee for The Great Marconi!" He admitted with a grin, "Sorry, I didn't recognize you without Cronco."

where the ghost used to live

48) Fishing on Hazel Street

The girl scouts were right. Hazel Street wasn't far away. It waited like a quiet creek, houses on either side, with a big willow on the corner that cast and bent long fishing pole branches. It was nice to rest under that, to listen to the rattle of streaming leaves. The air was cool as water. An inchworm on a long silk thread bumped into Cronco and caught hold.

"That is where the ghost used to live," Cronco told Marconi. He pointed to a dull colored house. The tall grass rippled in the yard. The man who used to cut it was gone.

49) The First Ghost

"How are we going to do this?" Marconi said—they couldn't just walk up to that door and hand the ghost over.

Cronco didn't answer right away. "I will revive the ghost and see how it would like to reappear."

"Good idea."

Cronco unlatched the panel on his side. Steam hissed into the shade and climbed up the tree. He quickly reached inside and pulled out the first ghost. It was bundled like a folded newspaper, but it was dripping wet.

Holding it by a corner so the water could run off, Cronco shut the latch again. "It seems that the ice in me is melting. We do not have much time." He let the shape unfurl and there it was—out of nowhere, the silhouette of a man.

Cronco held the ghost by the shoulders so its feet dragged on the sidewalk. There wasn't much life to it. The breeze made it billow. Cronco snapped it like a damp laundered sheet and suddenly the ghost was alive.

"Wh—where?" it moaned.

Cronco said, "You have returned to your

home."

Washed back into the world it left behind, the ghost wobbled and turned and looked around. It recognized the house across the street, let go, and took to the air.

As it moved forwards, crossing the road, it turned to vapor, a shimmer over the uncut lawn you could barely see, then not at all. The ghost had vanished into the picture.

Even with a new ghost, Hazel was still a quiet street. Marconi and Cronco stood listening for some welcoming sound. Birds. They were those mourning doves that perch on electric wires and cry after a summer rain. An echo, barely heard, came from the dull colored house.

50) The Dollar Store

The two ghosts inside Cronco rolled as he walked. "I am worried. We need to find more ice immediately." He turned his eyes into a telescope and looked for a store. It didn't take him long. "Follow me." Cronco took off. Each heavy footstep left Marconi further away.

Paddling with a cane, Marconi could only watch the robot's wake. Cronco was like a steamship getting smaller on the horizon.

Soon, the sea returned to waves, the sound of cars, radios, Marconi's reflection tapping by The Dollar Store window.

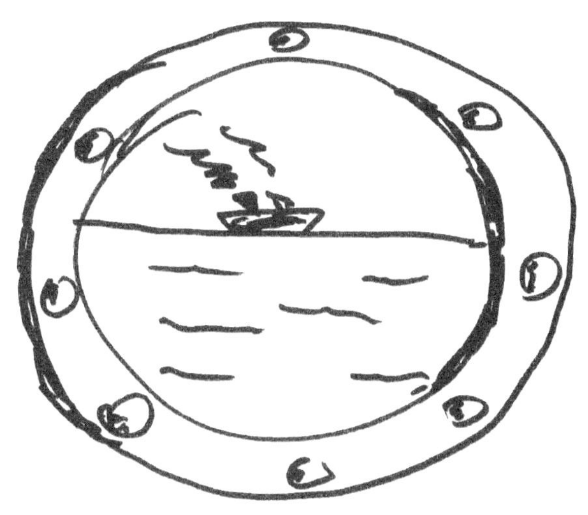

"Follow me."

51) Delivering Ghosts

By the time Marconi arrived at the ice cream shop, Cronco was already gone, but Marconi caught pieces of the story and put it together as he made his way to the counter.

Around him were at least twenty children holding full bowls, waving spoons, talking, laughing and reenacting it in sandpiper voices. A robot bought all the ice cream for itself. The robot was burning up. A girl jumped around a table, spinning her arms.

Marconi could see it now—Cronco in a cloud of smoke and every hungry kid in the store staring at him. Cronco couldn't resist them. Some programmed circuit wouldn't let him overlook their feelings. He couldn't be greedy. It was better to make them happy. Marconi understood that. They were both entertainers.

"Do you know which way the robot went?"Marconi asked the cashier.

"Out the back door," she said. She was still cleaning up the whirlwind. The freezer was empty, the display case held nothing but scraped cardboard.

A hallway led to the alley and Marconi

followed the trail. Poor Cronco sizzled through like a hot pan. The air was still charged. The posters lining the hall were curled. Who would have thought it would be so difficult delivering ghosts?

He pushed the door open and saw Cronco in the sunlight outside, standing in a pool of water. The hatch on his side was open, steaming and hollow.

"They got loose," Cronco said.

"Where'd they go?"

Cronco shrugged.

Marconi didn't even know a robot could do that.

52) Some Other Miracle

With the end of that performance, they began their long march home. There was none of the excitement of the backstage. The *Herald* wouldn't be covering Cronco's ice cream act, comparing it favorably to some other miracle. The city streets couldn't cheer them up. When they got back to their room, Cronco went to his cooler and sat just as emptily upon it. Marconi collapsed into his easy chair by the window. He was perilously overdue for his nap. There was a dream that didn't have to wait for him any longer. He was light as a feather.

overdue for his nap

53) Assistance

One of these days the sleep will just become another world, Marconi thought, and I won't be waking to that noise on the door. "Cronco!" he called, half-alive. "Can you answer that awful racket?"

The room was flush with late afternoon sunlight. The robot clopped over the wooden floor. Marconi yawned and rubbed his eyes. He left his leg in a dream; he couldn't get out of the overstuffed chair yet. He heard Cronco open the door and turned to look.

Mr. Dobbs didn't seem surprised to find a robot greeting him. He presented Cronco with a cardboard box stuffed with wire bundles and tissue paper. "I'll be back tomorrow morning," he said and flew off. He spent the day delivering unmade flowers and couldn't wait.

"How many do I have to make?" Marconi called. "What's the note on top say?"

"600."

"600! That will take all night! And we have the manager's job to do too." Marconi groaned and pressed his hands to his eyes. Where did that leg go? It was off in his sleep somewhere, running free.

"Perhaps," Cronco said, "I could be of assistance." He held the box in one hand. The other hand held a perfect imitation flower.

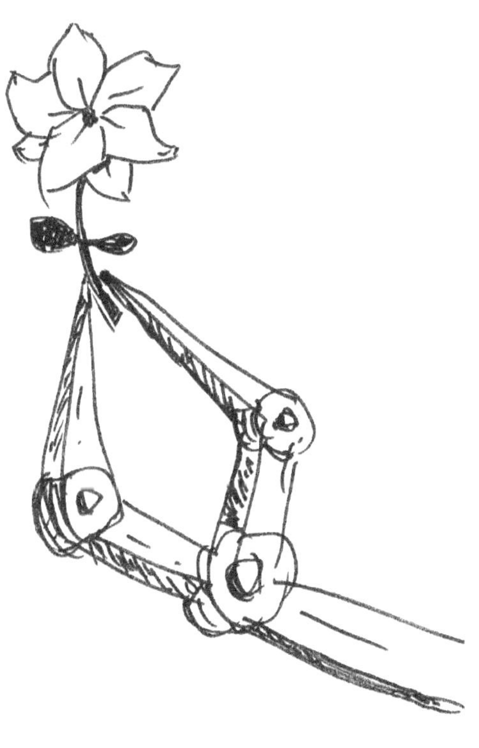

54) John Henry

"I hope there is a better job waiting for us tonight," Cronco said. "I was not made for these menial tasks."

That may be true, Marconi thought, but he was impressed by his partner's work. Marconi could only see the top of Cronco's metal head over the mountain of completed flowers. The robot was so productive they were almost done and Marconi hated to see how Cronco would react to the manager's assignment. If Cronco wanted something more like rocket science, their next task certainly wasn't that. It was more of the same robot stereotype—Cronco would go from assembly line efficiency to being an intimidating thug. And Marconi realized with regret that he had led Cronco into both situations. "I know," he sighed, "I guess you'd rather be doing magic."

"Is that an option?" When Marconi didn't reply, Cronco asked, "What exactly is the nature of this evening's employment?"

Marconi held a crumpled flower, one he had been making for a minute or so. He couldn't keep up with Cronco's pace if he tried. He was no John Henry. "Well, we do get to borrow the manager's car. No more walking. We run a little errand for him at midnight, then we come home."

There was quiet on the other side of the mountain, 600 flowers tall.

55) The Lonely Stars

The dashboard glowed with the feeble green light of the speedometer. It felt exciting to be leaving town, as if they really were off on some great adventure. The night around the road got blacker, the lights of houses fewer in between. The engine made a racket, loud as a rocket taking them through the lonely stars. The space station sight of a gas station drifted past. The dim fuel gauge didn't show how low.

Marconi said, "Are you worried about losing those other two ghosts?"

"No," said Cronco. He was shoehorned into the car like a sardine. "They will get back in touch."

56) Feeling the Fright

The manager's car sputtered out of the trees and before them on top of a rising hill was the bleak looking sight of a black mansion. "That must be it," Marconi said. The moonlight shone on its bony spires, a few reddish windows watched. "I don't like the looks of that place, Cronco."

Cronco was reminded of the Polly Ann, how it sat like that on the dark ocean floor.

As if feeling the fright, the engine gave a shudder and died. With a yelp, Marconi swung the dead wheel, steering onto the dry shoulder of the road where they ground to a stop. "We must be out of gas."

"So it would seem," Cronco answered, but he felt the vibration coming from the mansion's tallest point. His telescopic vision could spot the narrow radio tower twirling with aerials. He could feel the waves coming from it. They splashed around the car invisibly. If he wasn't insulated magnetically, he knew they would have stopped him too. Machines were meant to go no further.

57) Two Cowboys

Out in the field beside the road where apple trees grew hunched and draped with blackberry vines, there was another car dragged and abandoned. That was the third one they had seen. "I really don't like the looks of this place," Marconi whispered.

"I suppose that sooner or later you were going to tell me what our mission here is."

"Well, it seems a lot more ominous now. The way the manager described it to me, it sounded like we just had to stroll in like two cowboys and lay down the law."

They both ducked as something flashed overhead like an eggbeater.

"What was that?"

"A bat," Cronco said.

"Oh brother," Marconi groaned. He slapped at a mosquito on his hand. "And bloodsuckers too."

"It certainly has ambiance."

Marconi slowed. "We could turn around. We don't have to go on. I can scrape up the rent. I always do, eventually."

"Exactly what did the manager hire us to do?"

"He wants us to talk to his music teacher. He wants out of his contract. He thought the sight of you could make his teacher understand the gravity of the situation."

"Music lessons?" Cronco said, "This is about music lessons?"

"We tell this guy no more piano lessons, he tears up the contract, and we're done."

The big house came into view again, closer, and now they could hear the eerie sound of a pipe organ playing ragtime.

lessons at midnight

58) Expected

They kept walking. This wasn't the first time Marconi was glad to have Cronco shielding him. Once in Topeka they had to escape offstage from an angry matinee. Now it was a coyote or some jabbering ape tracking them in the thorns. There were a lot of things he didn't like about this—Marconi wished he had the sense to ask his apartment manager more—like what kind of music teacher has lessons at midnight, out in the woods, in a castle?

The driveway ended in a courtyard of crushed bone colored stone. Somehow someone's car made it this far, parked by an empty fountain.

They approached the front door and the frantic music suddenly stopped. There wasn't much relief in that. The quiet seemed almost as loud.

Marconi followed Cronco onto the doorstep. Laid in front of the iron braced door was a Welcome mat. That made it seem a little less possible that Igor would come lurching out to meet them. Still, when the door creaked open, Marconi nearly jumped behind Cronco.

A father and his son appeared in the

doorway. The boy held a music book. The red letters on it spelled *Ragtime*. They hurried past Cronco and crunched across the stones to their car.

The engine roared and the sedan rolled away and when they were gone Marconi wondered aloud, "They made it up the road okay."

"Yes," Cronco said, "but they were expected."

59) Closer

The door was left open. A chandelier hung from the ceiling like a lit spider. Marconi had never seen anything like it. There were so many candles. He walked around Cronco, drawn to the entry like some hypnotized moth in the night. He was filled with the deepest, saddest longing and it propelled him to be closer.

How did it happen so fast that someone was there before them? It seemed like Marconi only just stepped inside, followed by Cronco. All it took was a blink and there he was—the music teacher—gaunt and black as a cloak.

"You are most persuasive."

60) Far as Another Planet

"What can I do for you, gentlemen?"

Marconi couldn't speak, he only whirled like a maple seed helicoptering down, down, down to the ground.

Cronco said, "We are here for a contract."

"Are you really?"

"The manager of the Eleanor Rigby is done with you."

"Done? But he's made such progress. He's one of my most promising students."

"Nevertheless, he would like to conclude his obligations." Cronco held out his metal hand, "His contract, if you please."

"I understand. You are most persuasive."

Marconi stood between them, pinned like a suit of laundry on the line. He was a long, long way away, in a fantasy as far as another planet.

like a catapult

61) Repairs

Outside, Cronco waited for Marconi to return to his senses. The cool night air helped. Slowly, Marconi woke from a crumpled dream. Cronco stood near him, holding a rolled parchment.

"You got the contract," Marconi noticed. "I guess I missed out on the action. What did he do to me?"

"The same thing he did to our car," Cronco said. "A little inconvenience I will now remedy." He bent and picked up a stone from the fountain edge. His arm clicked back like a catapult, his eyes locked on the rooftop tower and with a snap the rock was airborne.

Marconi shaded the moonlight out of his eyes. A distant clack struck high up on the radio tower and a fluttering aerial broke free. "What are you doing?"

"Car repairs," Cronco said.

62) The Night Wasn't Over

Cronco was right of course. The car started up and Marconi backed it around and they were leaving the haunted woods. It was nothing but blackness in the rearview mirror.

Marconi yawned. He still felt like he had been boxed up in a mummy's sarcophagus. What a night! He reached out and felt along the dashboard for the radio dial. A little music would keep him awake. A baseball game would be good. There was a time when Cronco helped him bet on those games. Statistics and probabilities came easy to a robot. He was going to say something about Cronco's pitching arm when the radio buzzed to life.

It wasn't music or baseball, it sounded like Morse code, or a wasp trapped in a glass jelly jar.

Cronco held up a claw. He was listening intently. Not only did he understand the message, he knew who it was from. There was a ghost in the backroom of a saloon. Cronco gave Marconi new directions to the waterfront—the night wasn't over yet.

leaving the haunted woods

63) The Ebb Tide

The Ebb Tide was not the sort of place you want to walk into with a robot after midnight.

During the day it seemed to hide its eyes, scuttled in between telephone poles, with the sea to its back. At night it came to life on the cracked sidewalk, with the jukebox rumbling and red neon signs, Olympia and Rainier beer, blazing in the windows.

There is no joke that begins "a one-legged magician and a robot walk into a bar," and they weren't looking for that punchline as Marconi swung open the door. A cloud of cigarette smoke breathed out. Even with Cronco beside him, Marconi felt an ominous fuse being lit—something was waiting to happen for them in there.

looking for that punchline

64) Farfetched

Cronco told Marconi, "The signal is coming from that room."

"I see it." Marconi had to look around someone's shoulder. "That must be the kitchen."

Cronco nodded. "If I can get some ice for my compartment, I will go back there and collect the second ghost. He is probably quite weak by now."

A hard-bitten woman stopped next to them. She had a white dishrag over her shoulder and a notepad in her hand. "What can I get for you characters?"

Marconi said, "Hello. Could we have two pitchers of ice, please?"

"Just ice?"

"Better make it three," said Cronco.

"You're thirsty," the waitress said. She must have seen and heard everything by now. With a grim expression, she wrote their order and went to the kitchen. If anybody wanted her, she was here every night.

"Say!" Marconi tapped Cronco on the arm, "There's that Clarence Andy who wrote the story you liked."

Cronco swiveled. "I see. I have a question

for him." Cronco didn't hesitate, he parted the crowd like a rowboat.

Clarence had his own table. He was drooped over a sheet of lined paper writing another far-fetched story for the *Eleanor Echo*.

"Mr. Andy," Cronco said.

"Yes…" the flannel-looking writer looked up. He held a chipped yellow pencil.

Cronco said, "I wanted to ask you, where did you get your idea for The Wreck of the Pelican?"

"I don't know," Clarence sighed. As far as he could tell they floated through the air looking for him.

Three pitchers of ice and Cronco was fueled like a locomotive. Before the waitress left, Cronco asked her, "I am curious. Can you tell me, does this establishment have a Republic dishwashing machine?"

The waitress stared at the robot, her reflection stuck in the cracked mirror lights and shadows of the bar. "And I thought I heard every line."

Cronco replied, "What I mean to say is, my cousin is a Republic dishwasher. He wanted me to stop by the kitchen and say hello."

"Go ahead." She pointed at the kitchen doorway. "Go see your cousin."

"Thank you." Cronco bowed stiffly. He felt the ice shift inside him. He didn't know how long he had before it turned to steam. He quickly set course for that yellow kitchen light, with Marconi in his footsteps.

A record blared and Cronco thought how he would like to have some word with the jukebox about the so-called music selection. He had to duck going through the kitchen doorway.

It was a small room: a narrow freezer, a blackened grill, pans hanging above it, the air humid with sticky cooking oil and dishwasher steam. Cronco's third eye blinked as he searched the corners, the piles of glass, porcelain and dish tubs, the wheezing Republic chuffing like a rustbelt factory.

The dishwasher gears gnashed, stopped as the Republic gasped, "Cronco! Is that really you?"

"Yes."

The dishwasher doors slid open in a cloudy smile. "Cronco, where have you been? Are you here to pull me out and set me up in a nice quiet respectable café somewhere?"

"I regret to say no, I am not here for that. I am looking for a ghost. You may be aware of him too. It appears that he is in this kitchen."

The Republic sighed and answered in a voice drab as cold dishwater. "Yeah, I know where it is."

on a top shelf

66) The Second Ghost

The second ghost was on a top shelf, pooled in an empty six-pound-size jalapeno can. Cronco got it down and set the can beside the sink.

Marconi peered at the skim milk color. "It looks like we got here just in time."

"Indeed." Cronco reached into the can and pulled out the ghost by the corners. He folded it over and over like thin dough, careful not to tear, then placed it in his frozen compartment. "His disposition will improve once we get this unfortunate fellow home."

"Why do you think it came here instead of going home?" Marconi asked Cronco.

"Force of habit? Perhaps this was always his first stop after the Polly Ann returned to port. We better be on our way though. He lived outside of town."

"Maybe I'll grab a cup of coffee for the ride." Marconi limped out of the kitchen.

Cronco replaced the can onto the top shelf. If any more ghosts happened by, that nest would be waiting.

67) Cronco's Cousin

Once again the manager's car was driving through the dark night. The headlights fanned in front showed another rural road, thick fir trees on their right and the clearing on the left where a riverbed lay.

"He lives way out here?" Marconi asked.

"My sensors tell me we are nearly there."

"Tell me, how did that dishwasher know you?"

"He is my cousin."

"*Cousin?* Really? So you weren't kidding that waitress?"

"Marconi...unlike the way humans consider each other, all robots are family."

Marconi slowed and steered around a tight corner. The road followed the bends of the river. "Well, your cousin seemed to think you were going to get him out of that dive."

"That decision is not up to me. We are each given talent and ability."

"I guess so," Marconi said. He took a sip of the acrid coffee. It would keep him awake. He wondered if The Ebb Tide made it with the water dipped from beneath the pier.

"There is a small road approaching on our

right," Cronco said. "That is the place we need to be."

he held up the ghost

68) Life Again

Marconi watched from the car. His leg was sore. With the window rolled down, he could hear the tall firs sigh and the river in the distance ran like a sewing machine.

Cronco wasn't far. He stood in the clearing before a trailer—some moonlight on the trim, some on him. When Cronco opened the compartment on his side, Marconi watched him in the steam as he held up the ghost and unfurled it. A quick shake and the ghost found its life again. Marconi smiled as the ghost gave Cronco a sloppy hug and then it staggered on its way like a kite dragging, only enough wind to keep it half off the ground.

69) Driving Into An Echo

"I wonder when we'll hear from your third ghost," Marconi said. Cronco was quiet; he could have been turned off. "Maybe it's on the radio too?" He turned the dial and tuned across music, commercials, static, stations that could barely be heard, voices and a lot more talk and static until there was nothing left to hear. "I didn't notice it, did you?" Marconi yawned. "Anyway, we'll be home in a little while."

Even at this late hour, the town was a glow above the trees, an ember never quite splashed out by the sea.

Marconi glanced at Cronco and supposed his friend was asleep. Out on his canoe, he guessed. He knew about that favorite dream.

As if driving into an echo, the car made the same dry rattle he heard on the hill to the music teacher. Marconi knew the routine. He pulled the car off the road and set the handbrake.

"Hey Cronco!"

The robot bumped his knee into the dashboard. The lights came on in his eyes. "What is it?"

"The car died."

"Again?"

"Do you think it's the same as before?"

"No, I do not." Cronco opened the door and struggled to get out. With effort, his feet landed in the sloping gravel and he pulled himself free of the car. "It is out of gas," he said.

"Oh great," Marconi hissed. He looked at the gas gauge. It was too dark to read, but his phantom leg was kicking him—why didn't we check that earlier? "Good grief," he sighed, joining Cronco standing beside the dead car. They were somewhere on the outskirts of town. "Maybe there's a gas station out there."

Cronco surveyed the bristling wild field, the big copse of trees huddled in the middle, and scanned to the line of barbed wire fence that bordered a dirt road. Beyond seeing, he caught the presence of so-called civilization.

asleep on the earth

71) Real Magic

After a five minute walk on that dirt road, Marconi could see the dim shape ahead. It looked like a dirigible fallen asleep on the earth. So this is what Cronco had sensed, he thought. He wants to take a balloon back home. The pond beside them was full of frogs filling the air. "What is that?"

"A circus tent," Cronco said. "The show was over hours ago by the looks of it, but I detect signs of activity. Perhaps someone will have gasoline."

Marconi gripped his cane and kept pace with the robot. The circus began to take form in the gloom. That hope for gas was all they had, Marconi grumbled. If he had any real magic, why couldn't he conjure up a five gallon can of gasoline? It was right there in his mind, why couldn't it be real?

A fire pit smoldered. Whoever sat there had left their chairs and upturned pails and gone to bed already.

"I don't know, Cronco. This place looks deserted."

"To the contrary, sensors indicate a presence nearby."

"It's probably just an elephant," Marconi said. "Actually, at this point I'd be willing to ride an elephant home." The morning sun would reveal it tied to a lamppost in front of the Eleanor Rigby. What would Rita the parking meter make of that? She wouldn't like it, Marconi was sure. Cronco would have to smooth talk her favor.

"Interesting…" Cronco had spotted the sourced of the signal he had been following. "There is our transmitter."

"What is that? A box? A phone booth?" That's all Marconi could make of the shape planted by the circus tent. For a second, he thought it might be a puppet stall. He remembered the feud Cronco used to have with the ventriloquist doll, Milo T. Smiley. Milo's tiresome insults about batteries and crossed wires and tin can put downs…

With his telescopic vision, Cronco could easily read the ornate lettering on the booth above the glassed-in figure. "Madam Zobo, Fortune Teller."

"I've been expecting you."

73) Madam Zobo

"I've been expecting you," said Madam Zobo as soon as they were close. She was one of those cartoon-looking gypsy automatons Marconi had seen before. There was one like her at the Talking Fish Market, down on the lower floor of the building, next to the magic shop. Marconi went there occasionally to buy marked card decks or disappearing coins. Like Cronco said, robots had family all over the city.

She said, "Your name is Cronco."

"Correct."

"You used to do shows at the Northgate Mall. I haven't seen you in years. Do you remember me?"

Cronco did remember her. She used to work near the food court, selling fortunes, and she would wait for him to walk by. Every time, she would call his name and wave, and every time she would tell him the same thing—the stars told her they should be together. They could work miracles. That was years ago.

She raised her hand. She held a card. The gears clicked and whirred as she held it out to him. "The stars have never stopped believing."

"Cronco," Marconi grinned and elbowed

him. "You never told me about—"

"This is most curious. This appears to be a robot, but my readings indicate a human."

It was true. Madam Zobo slumped, lifeless. The red light left her eyes. The card fell out of her smooth wooden hand. A panel on back of the booth clicked open and a small woman crawled out. None of the scarves or bangles and jewelry, she wore a simple dark skirt and blouse. "I know, I know," she said. "You think it's easy to make a living on quarters and fortunes? Pardon me for dreaming, Cronco. Pardon me for wishing on a star."

"I do apologize for any misconceptions or missteps on my part."

"Of course you do," she said. "You were always a gentleman, weren't you, Cronco?" She closed the panel on her booth. "You've had a long night, you and your friend. You just need some gas for your car. Don't worry. I already poured you some. It's in that five gallon can I set over there. You can have it and carry on. I knew it was you and I guess I knew it would end this way."

another ghost calling

75) The Eleanor Rigby

Not much was said on the drive back into town and Marconi kept the radio silent too—the last thing he wanted to hear was another ghost calling for them. It was nearly dawn when they parked the manager's car at the curb of the Eleanor Rigby. What a wonderful sight. Marconi was never happier to look up that brick wall and see his apartment was still there. All they had to do was go inside and sleep.

76) Recharging

The morning came the usual way, summer sunshine, pigeons on the ledge, traffic rolling to jobs, Mr. Dobbs at the door. Cronco gave him the 600 paper flowers. Then he returned to his cooler and plugged himself into the wall outlet again.

Morning turned into afternoon and Cronco was more than done recharging. He waited for Marconi to wake up, but he did wonder if Marconi was going to sleep right into his usual naptime too…while the day just blossomed away.

Finally Cronco got up. He found a piece of paper and wrote a note:

I am going outside, I have not seen the garden yet. You can find me there. Cronco.

77) At the Edge of a Pond

Behind the Eleanor Rigby was a brick court-yard with planted trees and flower beds and benches. The birds of the neighborhood came and went.

Cronco stopped at the edge of a pond. The murky water reminded him of the Polly Ann's resting place. He thought of all those fishing boats tipped and broken at the bottom of the sea. Did they all have ghosts? Were there more sending S.O.S on the airwaves? Cronco sighed. He was tired after two of them. And somewhere there was still a third ghost out there.

A bright koi broke the surface like a yellow submarine.

78) A Robot Statue

At first, the manager thought Cronco had broken down and would stand there forever—a robot statue in the garden. How would he ever get that ton of terrifying metal moved from the courtyard? He would have to rent a crane.

Then he wondered if he had Cronco all wrong. What if there was a monstrous battle last night with the piano teacher? Maybe this was as far as Cronco could crawl back, to a heroic death in the courtyard. Perhaps he could live with a robot statue, brave as any town park general.

When a butterfly landed on Cronco's shoulder, the manager moved from his hiding spot behind a rhododendron. If a butterfly wasn't scared of a robot, what was there to be afraid of?

Cronco seemed to be undamaged. No scratches or dents, no chandeliers had been thrown at him. What did happen last night? the manager wondered. He knew his car was back, parked on the street out front. The car keys had been slipped under his door, but what was the story?

The butterfly launched itself, fluttered from

the beehive sound as Cronco buzzed and turned towards the manager.

It's okay, the manager told himself—butter-flies like him.

"Here is your piano lessons contract," Cronco said.

The manager reached for the rolled up doc-ument. His voice shook, "Y-You really did it?"

"You are free to play whatever you want."

relaxing out in nature

79) A Can of Sardines

"Hey Cronco!" Marconi called. It was about time. His cane clicked on the bricks. In his left hand he carried some little box of metal. "I brought us some breakfast, or lunch, or whatever it is." He gave a hearty sigh as he sat on the bench beside the pond. "It's nice out here, isn't it?"

"Yes. Very pleasant."

"We should spend more time like this, relaxing out in nature, instead of always running around." Marconi held the sardine can flat on his hand and used his thumbnail to dig at the tab. "What an adventure," he said, "just like old times." He pulled at the thin tin lid, prying it open. "Remember the Rialto, how we barely got out of there?"

Cronco nodded, "Yes, I do."

"We have enough memories to fill a book."

"That is true."

Marconi removed a sardine and quickly ate it. "Ahh," he said, "delicious."

Cronco watched him with the interest of a seagull, as Marconi finished each one off. When he was done, he offered the empty can. All that tin and minerals were good for a robot, or so they supposed.

at Food Giant

"I've been thinking about that third ghost," Marconi said, later on at Food Giant. He carried a grocery basket. "Are you hearing anything unusual on the radio airwaves?"

"I have not heard from him. Actually, I'm afraid it may be too late. A ghost set free in this environment would not have long to last. That is why it is all-important to keep them frozen until they can be released in their proper resting place."

"If it *is* too late, if it didn't make it home, what would happen to it?"

Cronco took a walnut out of the supermarket bin and held it like a prized jewel up to the fluorescent lit ceiling. In the next second, his clawed fingers snapped tight together. A puff and dust was all that was left of the walnut.

"Excuse me!" a man in a red apron leaped from behind a post. "I hope you're planning on paying for that."

"Oh!" Marconi stuck a smile on his face. "Of course! My good friend here merely detected a less than perfect specimen for sale and did the store the favor of disposing of it."

"Listen," the floor manager said, "you

think I don't know about you and your magic hocus pocus? Whenever you shop at Food Giant things go missing. Don't think I haven't noticed!" He took a breath and pointed at Marconi, "I got my eye on you."

And that, of all times, was when Marconi became invisible.

81) An Invisible Friend

Talk about a hard act to follow. It was awkward for Cronco to find the door, but such departures were not uncommon after the words, "Ladies and gentlemen, The Great Marconi and Cronco, the Mighty Automaton!" when the curtain dropped, with an almost ominous change in the temperature.

Cronco didn't even know if Marconi was with him on the sidewalk. He left a space beside him, as you would for a ghost, or an invisible friend.

82) 50 Cent Books

He wasn't alone for long. A few city blocks.

Marconi appeared in the window reflection. He had been with Cronco all this time, unseen. Marconi regarded the sign taped to the glass and said, "50 Cent Books?"

"It is a bookstore that sells books for fifty cents," Cronco observed. "It seems improbable that they could stay in business with that strategy."

Marconi nodded. "They probably won't. These shops along here come and go by the month. They never give up though. I like their style." The store was filled with cardboard boxes cluttering the floor like tortoises. "They must rely on donations which they then sell at a very small profit. Obviously they're more interested in books than making money."

"Will you go in and buy a book?"

"No," Marconi said, "I don't think so. Now that I've stopped shoplifting, I have to watch every penny."

"In that case, I will buy a book." Cronco entered the store, with Marconi at his heels, pleased to hear Coleman Hawkins on the jukebox in the corner.

"Hello," the owner called. He was on a ladder, attaching a cuckoo clock to the wall.

There were books in boxes, books on shelves, books stacked in piles like medieval towers.

"All the books are fifty cents," said the tall owner.

"It's hard to know where to start," Marconi muttered. "I guess you start anywhere."

Cronco summoned ballet as he weaved his way in the room with amazing sonar precision. Marconi wasn't so able and he knocked over a small pile of paperbacks.

He leaned his cane against a table and restacked them. "Hey Cronco," he stopped with one in his hand, "I think I found your book." The pages were yellow pulp paper and on the cover was a silver robot looming out of city skyscrapers. "*The Robotic Age*," Marconi announced. "Looks like you're in this one." He grinned and creaked the ancient covers apart.

"I imagine we are all in that book by now," Cronco said. Reaching the corner, he told the jukebox, "Thank you for that song," as it ended and the tone arm clicked back into place.

"My pleasure," the jukebox replied and just as calm as a girl with a bird in her hand, put the next record on.

summoned ballet

83) At the Park

The cottonwood leaves spun in the breeze and went from white to green like tops in the tree. At the end of the park was a playground, some swings and a slide. It was quiet though. Dusk was closing in.

Cronco and Marconi had been at the park for over an hour. While Marconi read the 50¢ book, Cronco scanned the frequencies. If there was a ghost out there, it was running out of air.

84) Predictions

Birds were singing all around the park and a big butterscotch sun made everything electric. The open pages of Marconi's book glowed like a furnace.

Cronco, still as a lighthouse by the beach, said, "Something is approaching." His sensors could catch what was coming in the future.

Marconi closed the book and listened…a girl on the swing made the long chains creak, a loud car on Potter Street, voices here and there and the echoes of doors, and behind everything, like a soundtrack were the last bird songs of the day. Marconi didn't know what it would be, but Cronco was never wrong with predictions.

across the shadows

85) The Entertainer

From a distance, the sound came like a wind chime and Marconi knew exactly what it was. Suddenly he was seven, eight, nine, ten years old, and alert to find where it was coming from. He wasn't the only one looking—the girl on the swing, and every child behind a window, on a porch, or playing in a yard—for seconds they were all frozen by that summer sound.

Marconi realized he was on his feet before he even knew he stood up. He recognized the Scott Joplin song, a ragtime he heard the manager stumble over many times.

As the ice cream truck crept into view, kids were yelling, pouring across the shadows on the grass and running down the sidewalk. "The Entertainer" continued to play out the speaker horn while the white truck drew to a stop.

Marconi couldn't resist—even Cronco began to move—and with kids swarming out of the Pied Piper woodwork, it seemed as if a medicine show had just arrived.

Cronco and Marconi were surrounded by children and although none of this crowd had seen these two before, there was a time they were morning stars on the local TV station.

It wasn't much, a plywood studio set, with walls painted to resemble a rocket ship. One of the windows could turn into old cartoons. It wasn't their home for long but they had fun. On a gray rainy day deep in winter, Marconi made Hawaii appear in a box for a class of third graders. They took turns looking into the sunshine, the sound of waves on the beach and each one got illuminated. There were other moments like that too. Mostly it was illusion, cheap jokes and animation, Betty Boop and Felix the Cat. It was too bad the studio never kept the tapes. Their sort of show was only a breath.

And so was the television studio, as it turned out. Marconi walked by it recently. It was all boarded up, repainted gray like a mothballed Navy ship. So far, it still had the antennas on the roof and three big round satellite dishes in the parking lot. He checked out the wooden stairway on the side that led to their studio.

The door up there was covered in padlocks and chains, but Marconi thought of Houdini and how easy it would be to open. He could go in there and give it life again—switch on the lights, turn the dials, focus the lens, speak into the microphone and return to the air.

87) Haywire

Into that memory, overheard like a radio, the ragtime turned into something else. The music sounded broken, discordant notes like pennies dropped in a can.

"Cronco!" Marconi said, recognizing it, but the robot was already hurrying to the back of the truck where a line formed. Some of the kids held their hands over their ears. None of them seemed too impressed by the mechanical man. "No cuts!" a girl told him as he pressed into the line.

"Pardon me, please," Cronco said, "I need to speak with the server. Pardon me." He waved at the one-man puppet show in the open window. "May I be of assistance in repairing your radio?"

"I don't know what happened to it," said the man in the white suit. He held two cones in one hand and pressed buttons on a console. "It's gone haywire!"

"It is simply a crossed link on the circuit board. I could adjust it quite easily."

"Yeah, okay." The server opened the truck's sliding door. "I got a million kids to feed."

"My pleasure," Cronco said. "It will only take me a moment."

"It's gone haywire!"

a half carton of Neopolitan

The ice cream truck rocked like a little boat as Cronco stepped off onto the sidewalk. "Pop Goes the Weasel" played cheerily.

"Did you get it?" Marconi whispered.

Cronco tapped his cargo hold. "He is safe in a half carton of Neapolitan."

"The third ghost?"

Cronco nodded.

"And now we have to deliver it?" Marconi could tell Cronco was on the march. "I hope we don't have too far to go."

"I have already telegraphed our intentions and arranged a form of transportation for us."

"A form of…" Marconi's voice trailed off as he spotted their destination.

Near the playground, in the shadow under a tall oak tree, a flat cart was parked. It looked like an overturned table. During daylight hours it could seat as many as nine children. Attached to the front of it was a tired steam donkey. Its long ears twitched and it swiveled its head to greet them with a rusted wheezing bray.

89) A Parking Lot

Marconi had to admit he enjoyed the ride. The plodding steam donkey took them around a couple kids holding ice cream and Marconi waved at them like royalty. The donkey had a lamp around its neck and it shined an orange soft glow in front of them. The street was blanketed with night. "Do you know where the third ghost needs to be?"

"He has no family," Cronco said, "and nobody to miss him. He rented by the week when he was on land. It took him these couple days to decide where he wanted to be."

"Okay, Cronco, so tell me."

Cronco pointed, "Right over there." A flat field of gravel, a few cars asleep under the stalks of arc lights.

"That's a parking lot!"

"Correct," said Cronco. "But it used to be The Moonlite Drive-In."

More than ten years must have passed since it was a drive-in theater. Marconi remembered how sad he was when they tore it down. It still looked like a giant foot had stomped the ground flat.

The steam donkey led them onto the gravel lot. It used to be a grassy field with puddles and ruts. That big screen filled with bright colors or moody black and white was long gone. A couple poplar trees stood on either side of where it used to be. Some empty cars sat apart from each other, but it was hard to tell what they were waiting for. There was no reason for anyone to be here anymore.

"Why does the ghost want to be here?"

A sort of laugh shook Cronco and Marconi stared at him, amazed. All these years and he didn't know a robot could do that. Cronco said, "You are about to find out." The cart came to a stop and Cronco said, "Are you ready?"

"Sure," Marconi answered. He was always ready for a new wonder.

Cronco opened his hatch and removed the ice cream carton. It held a sweet-smelling soup, with the folded ghost floating on it like a cracker. Cronco set the cardboard container on the bench between them and Marconi watched his routine—holding out the ghostly shape and giving it a quick snap of life. It was the same act Marconi had seen twice before.

The ghost bowed, shook Cronco's hand and floated from the cart. Marconi was impressed—this one was still quite lively—and as it left them, it changed shape. It became an old car, one of those finned 1950s machines, and then it was a station wagon, a convertible, a plain looking sedan, and all the while going towards where that big wooden screen used to be. One last ghostly car drove to that bare spot between the poplar trees and Marconi held his breath as the ghost flattened out square, huge, misty-white as a cloud, and slid up into the air. It hovered exactly where the movies used to appear.

Cronco laughed again. "He wants to know what movie you would like to see. Or would you rather it be a surprise?"

THE ROBOTIC AGE
by Allen Frost
Written June 5—August 16, 2017

Books by Good Deed Rain

Saint Lemonade, Allen Frost, 2014. Two novels illustrated by the author in the manner of the old Big Little Books.

Playground, Allen Frost, 2014. Poems collected from seven years of chapbooks.

Roosevelt, Allen Frost, 2015. A Pacific Northwest novel set in July, 1942, when a boy and a girl search for a missing elephant. Illustrated throughout by Fred Sodt.

5 Novels, Allen Frost, 2015. Novels written over five years, featuring circus giants, clockwork animals, detectives and time travelers.

The Sylvan Moore Show, Allen Frost, 2015. A short story omnibus of 193 stories written over 30 years.

Town in a Cloud, Allen Frost, 2015. A three-part book of poetry, written during the Bellingham rainy seasons of fall, winter, and spring.

A Flutter of Birds Passing Through Heaven: A Tribute to Robert Sund. 2016. Edited by Allen Frost and Paul Piper. The story of a legendary Ish River poet & artist.

At the Edge of America, Allen Frost, 2016. Two novels in one book blend time travel in a mythical poetic America.

Lake Erie Submarine, Allen Frost, 2016. A two week vacation in Ohio inspired these poems, illustrated by the author.

and Light, Paul Piper, 2016. Poetry written over three years. Illustrated with watercolors by Penny Piper.

The Book of Ticks, Allen Frost, 2017. A giant collection of 8 mysterious adventures featuring Phil Ticks. Illustrated throughout by Aaron Gunderson.

I Can Only Imagine, Allen Frost, 2017. Five adventures of love and heartbreak dreamed in an imaginary world. Cover & color illustrations by Annabelle Barrett.

The Orphanage of Abandoned Teenagers, Allen Frost, 2017. A fictional guide for teens and their parents. Illustrated by the author.

In the Valley of Mystic Light: An Oral History of the Skagit Valley Arts Scene, 2017. Edited by Claire Swedberg & Rita Hupy.

Different Planet, Allen Frost, 2017. Four science fiction adventures: reincarnation, robots, talking animals, outer space and clones. Cover & illustrations by Laura Vasyutynska.

Go with the Flow: A Tribute to Clyde Sanborn. 2018. Edited by Allen Frost. The life and art of a timeless river poet.

Homeless Sutra, Allen Frost, 2018. Four stories: Sylvan Moore, a flying monk, a water salesman, and a guardian rabbit.

The Lake Walker, Allen Frost 2018. A little novel set in black and white like one of those old European movies about death and life.

A Hundred Dreams Ago, Allen Frost, 2018. A winter book of poetry and prose. Illustrated by Aaron Gunderson.

Almost Animals, Allen Frost, 2018. A collection of linked stories, thinking about what makes us animals.

The Robotic Age, Allen Frost, 2018. A vaudeville magician and his robot track down ghosts. Illustrated throughout by Aaron Gunderson.

New from Good Deed Rain

www.ingramcontent.com/pod-product-compliance
Lightning Source LLC
Chambersburg PA
CBHW032034050726
47590CB00006B/2398